Baby Things

Elizabeth and Jessica were in their parents' bedroom. On Mrs. Wakefield's dresser was a book of wallpaper patterns. All the designs were of ducks, rainbows, and clouds.

"These are all for baby rooms!" Jessica said.

Elizabeth's eyes were round with surprise. "Do you think Mom's redecorating the guest room for a baby?" Elizabeth whispered.

Jessica's heart was racing. "That's what it looks like."

They looked at each other for a moment. "We're having a baby!" Jessica shouted, as she and Elizabeth jumped up and down.

Bantam Skylark Books in the SWEET VALLEY KIDS series

#1 SURPRISE! SURPRISE!
#2 RUNAWAY HAMSTER
#3 THE TWINS' MYSTERY TEACHER
#4 ELIZABETH'S VALENTINE
#5 JESSICA'S CAT TRICK
#6 LILA'S SECRET
#7 JESSICA'S BIG MISTAKE
#8 JESSICA'S ZOO ADVENTURE
#9 ELIZABETH'S SUPER-SELLING LEMONADE
#10 THE TWINS AND THE WILD WEST
#11 CRYBABY LOIS
#12 SWEET VALLEY TRICK OR TREAT
#13 STARRING WINSTON EGBERT
#14 JESSICA THE BABY-SITTER
#15 FEARLESS ELIZABETH
#16 JESSICA THE TV STAR
#17 CAROLINE'S MYSTERY DOLLS
#18 BOSSY STEVEN
#19 JESSICA AND THE JUMBO FISH
#20 THE TWINS GO TO THE HOSPITAL
#21 JESSICA AND THE SPELLING-BEE SURPRISE
#22 SWEET VALLEY SLUMBER PARTY
#23 LILA'S HAUNTED HOUSE PARTY
#24 COUSIN KELLY'S FAMILY SECRET
#25 LEFT-OUT ELIZABETH
#26 JESSICA'S SNOBBY CLUB
#27 THE SWEET VALLEY CLEANUP TEAM
#28 ELIZABETH MEETS HER HERO
#29 ANDY AND THE ALIEN
#30 JESSICA'S UNBURIED TREASURE
#31 ELIZABETH AND JESSICA RUN AWAY
#32 LEFT BACK!
#33 CAROLINE'S HALLOWEEN SPELL
#34 THE BEST THANKSGIVING EVER

SWEET VALLEY KIDS SUPER SNOOPER EDITIONS
#1 THE CASE OF THE SECRET SANTA
#2 THE CASE OF THE MAGIC CHRISTMAS BELL
#3 THE CASE OF THE HAUNTED CAMP

SWEET VALLEY KIDS

JESSICA THE BABY-SITTER

Written by
Molly Mia Stewart

Created by
FRANCINE PASCAL

Illustrated by
Ying-Hwa Hu

A BANTAM SKYLARK BOOK
NEW YORK · TORONTO · LONDON · SYDNEY · AUCKLAND

RL 2, ages 005–008

JESSICA THE BABY-SITTER
A Bantam Skylark Book / January 1991

Sweet Valley High® and Sweet Valley Kids are trademarks of
Francine Pascal

Conceived by Francine Pascal

Produced by Daniel Weiss Associates, Inc.
33 West 17th Street
New York, NY 10011

Cover art by Susan Tang

Skylark Books is a registered trademark of Bantam Books, a division of
Bantam Doubleday Dell Publishing Group, Inc.
Registered in U.S. Patent and Trademark Office and elsewhere.

ISBN 0-553-15838-4

Published simultaneously in the United States and Canada

Bantam Books are published by Bantam Books, a division of Bantam
Doubleday Dell Publishing Group, Inc. Its trademark, consisting of the
words "Bantam Books" and the portrayal of a rooster, is Registered in U.S.
Patent and Trademark Office and in other countries. Marca Registrada.
Bantam Books, 666 Fifth Avenue, New York, New York 10103.

PRINTED IN THE UNITED STATES OF AMERICA

OPM   12   11   10   9   8   7   6   5   4   3   2

To Kimberly Bloom

CHAPTER 1

The New Neighbor

Elizabeth Wakefield picked up her books the moment the school bus stopped. "Hurry up, Jess!" she called to her twin sister Jessica. "Mom says we can visit Mrs. DeVito's new baby today!"

"I know," Jessica answered. She followed her sister down the aisle and jumped from the last step onto the sidewalk. "I can't wait to meet her."

Elizabeth walked quickly. "Mom says she had blond hair and blue eyes, just like us."

Elizabeth and Jessica both had blue-green

eyes and long blond hair with bangs. Everything about the way they looked was the same, because they were identical twins. They were the only identical twins at Sweet Valley Elementary School.

Being twins was fun. Sometimes they could tell what the other was thinking. Sometimes they even finished each other's sentences. The two girls sat next to each other in their second-grade class at school. At home, they shared a bedroom. They loved being twins. Elizabeth and Jessica were best friends.

Just because they looked the same on the outside didn't mean they were identical on the inside. Elizabeth and Jessica had many different interests. Elizabeth liked reading and playing outdoor games such as pirates or space explorers. Jessica hated to get messy, so she liked to play inside with her dolls and stuffed animals. She didn't like doing homework very much, either, but Elizabeth was always glad to help.

"I'll bet she looks like an angel," Jessica said happily. "That's what Grandma Wakefield says babies look like."

Behind them, their older brother Steven began to laugh. "An angel? Give me a break!" he said, making a horrible face.

"Boys just don't understand," Jessica said in her most grown-up voice. She led the way up the front walk and into the Wakefield house.

"Hi, kids!" Mrs. Wakefield called out.

"Can we really go see Mrs. DeVito's new baby?" Jessica asked as she rushed into the kitchen.

Mrs. Wakefield was working on a project for her decorating class. She had wallpaper samples spread out on the kitchen table. "As soon as you've had your snack, we'll go over and see her."

"Does she have a name yet?" Elizabeth asked.

"They named her Jennifer, but they call her Jenny," their mother said with a smile.

"That's a beautiful name," Jessica said. "Let's hurry so we can go see Jennifer De-Vito."

Jessica and Elizabeth had some cookies and milk, and then they walked to the De-Vitos' house with Mrs. Wakefield. Mrs. De-Vito answered the door.

"Hello!" she said happily. "Did you come to meet your new neighbor?"

4

Elizabeth nodded. "Congratulations," she said.

"Thank you," Mrs. DeVito answered. "Come on in. Jenny just woke up from her nap."

Jessica ran into the living room and saw a baby basket on the table. She walked over quietly and peeked in. Jenny DeVito was as small and perfect as a little doll. She looked up at them with her light blue eyes and blinked sleepily.

"Oh!" Jessica gasped. "She's so cute!"

Elizabeth smiled from ear to ear. "Look at how tiny her toes are!"

"Can I hold her?" Jessica whispered. "I'll be very, very careful."

Mrs. Wakefield started to shake her head, but Mrs. DeVito nodded. "I'll show you how," she said.

Elizabeth held her breath while Mrs. De-Vito picked Jenny up and placed her in Jessica's outstretched arms. Jenny waved one tiny fist in the air and gurgled.

"You have to support her head," Mrs. De-Vito said. "Just put one hand right under it."

"Like this?" Jessica asked, cradling Jenny's head gently. Her eyes sparkled. "She's just like a baby doll."

Jenny burped, and everyone laughed.

"Except most dolls don't do that," Elizabeth said with a laugh.

"Wouldn't it be fun to have a baby sister?" Jessica said softly. "We could dress her up and play with her, just like a doll."

Elizabeth shrugged. Playing with dolls wasn't her favorite thing to do. But it might be fun to have a baby sister.

"I think it would be wonderful," Jessica whispered.

Before anyone could answer, Jenny frowned and burped again.

"I guess she needs a little pat on the back," Mrs. DeVito said. She took Jenny back and put her against her shoulder. "Thank you all for coming to visit."

As the Wakefields headed for the door, Elizabeth glanced at her sister. From the look on Jessica's face, Elizabeth could tell that Jessica was thinking about something and that it was something big. She knew that before very long she would know what Jessica's big plan was.

CHAPTER 2

Two of Everything

"I got to hold Jenny," Jessica told her father at dinner. "She's adorable."

"I'll bet she is," Mr. Wakefield said.

Mrs. Wakefield poured milk for Elizabeth and Jessica. "Jenny really is darling," she agreed. "She reminds me of you girls when you were tiny babies just home from the hospital."

"I'll bet Jenny won't be as much of a handful as *two* wiggly twins," Mr. Wakefield said with a laugh.

Elizabeth grinned. "Were we really a handful, Daddy?"

Mr. Wakefield made such a funny face that everyone laughed.

"We had two strollers, two cribs, two of everything," Mrs. Wakefield said.

"And I was always sure we were getting you two mixed up," Mr. Wakefield added.

Jessica's eyes widened. "Maybe I'm really Elizabeth!" she said.

"And maybe I'm really Jessica," Elizabeth went on.

"You're too much of a tomboy to be Jessica," Steven reminded her.

Mrs. Wakefield smiled at Jessica and Elizabeth. "Of course we knew who was who. You each have different personalities. We dressed you in different outfits from the very beginning, so you would each be individuals. Babies are so wonderful," she went on. "They even smell nice."

Steven grabbed his throat. "Yuck!" he gasped. "Babies smell awful. I had to hold my nose all the time when they were babies." He demonstrated by pinching his nose and squeezing his eyes shut.

"Oh, really?" Mr. Wakefield asked. "You remember when they were babies? You were just a little two-year-old sprout, yourself."

"I do remember," Steven said firmly. "It was terrible."

Jessica frowned at him. "We were not terrible, Steven. You're just making it up."

"I remember that you were very happy to have two little sisters," Mrs. Wakefield said to Steven.

"No way," Steven muttered. "I hated every minute of it."

Elizabeth stuck her tongue out at him and then grinned to show she didn't mean it.

"And right from the beginning, you two talked to each other in your own language," Mrs. Wakefield continued. "It sounded like 'goo-boo-ba-ba' to me, but you both seemed to know just what you were talking about."

"Did we really talk to each other?" Jessica asked. It was fun hearing about what they had been like as babies.

Mr. Wakefield nodded. "I used to hear you two every morning before I went in to change you."

"That's right. It sounded like this," Steven said. He took a deep breath and yelled, "Waaaaah!"

Mrs. Wakefield laughed. "You know, Steven, you even tried to talk in their baby language."

Steven's face got red. "I did not."

"Yes, you did," Mrs. Wakefield continued. "You used to stand over their cribs and talk to them."

Jessica and Elizabeth both giggled. "What did you want to tell us?" Elizabeth asked him.

"Nothing," Steven began.

"You showed them all your toys," Mrs. Wakefield said with a tender smile.

Steven's face got even redder. "I did not."

"Yes, you did," Mr. Wakefield said. His brown eyes were twinkling with laughter. "You put your favorite bunny rabbit in Jessica's crib once."

13

Jessica couldn't help laughing at how embarrassed Steven was. "Thanks, Steven," she said.

Steven twirled his spaghetti on his fork and didn't say anything.

"It really was fun having two babies at once," Mrs. Wakefield said. "I can't believe how grown-up you two are now. I sometimes miss having two babies around."

Jessica smiled. Having a new baby for a neighbor was going to be lots of fun. She really wished they could have a new baby of their own. That would be a hundred times better.

CHAPTER 3

A Baby Sister

Elizabeth and Jessica walked together to the bus stop the next morning. Elizabeth was balancing her books on top of her head.

"Look over there," Jessica said, pointing across the street.

"Where?" Elizabeth turned her head, and her books fell. She didn't see anything except a woman pushing a stroller.

"A baby," Jessica said dreamily.

Elizabeth looked at her sister. "So?"

"Don't you wish we could have a baby

sister?" Jessica asked. "I wish, I wish, I wish we could have a baby sister."

Elizabeth thought for a moment. "It would be fun to have a baby sister or a baby brother. It wouldn't make any difference to me if it was a boy or a girl," she said.

"We could dress her up in the pretty baby dresses we used to wear," Jessica went on. "We could play dolls with her and brush her hair."

"It would be fun having a baby brother, too," Elizabeth pointed out. "We could teach him to play catch and to make forts and things outside."

"I wouldn't want another brother," Jessica said.

"What?" Steven said, running up behind them. "What are you talking about?"

17

"None of your beeswax!" Jessica said.

Elizabeth shrugged. "We were talking about what it would be like to have a baby brother or sister," she said.

"If Mom is going to have a baby, it better be a boy. I'm sick of having sisters," Steven said.

"Let's try to get Mom to have a baby," Jessica whispered when Steven walked away.

"How are we supposed to do that?" Elizabeth said with a laugh. "What if she doesn't want to have another baby?"

Jessica folded her arms stubbornly. "Don't you remember how much she liked Jenny DeVito? At dinner all she talked about was how cute and cuddly babies are."

"That's true," Elizabeth said. "Do you

think we really could talk her into having another baby?"

Jessica grinned. "Sure we can. All we have to do is make her keep remembering how much she likes babies, and then she'll want to have another one."

Elizabeth tucked her books under her arm as their bus came down the street. "I knew you had a plan up your sleeve. I could tell when we left Mrs. DeVito's house. It *would* be really nice if we had a baby brother or sister."

"We can do it," Jessica said confidently. "Starting this afternoon, let's start talking her into it, OK?"

Smiling, Elizabeth nodded and got in line for the bus. "It's a deal."

19

CHAPTER 4

Pickle Ice Cream!

Jessica took her sandwich out of her lunch bag and looked around the table. She waited until there was a quiet moment.

"Our neighbor has a new baby," she announced. "We saw her yesterday."

Ellen Riteman and Eva Simpson both gasped. "You did?" Eva asked. "Is she really sweet and tiny?"

"Yes, she looks just like an angel," Jessica said proudly.

"Babies don't look like angels, they look

like tiny bald people with red faces," Lila Fowler said with a giggle.

Amy Sutton and Elizabeth both laughed.

"Jenny is really cute," Elizabeth said. "And she's not bald. She has very light blond hair."

"You know," Ellen spoke up. "I think Andy Franklin's mom is having a baby soon."

Jessica looked down the lunch table. "Hey, Andy!" she shouted.

"Is your mother going to have a baby?" Ellen added.

Andy nodded. "I'm glad I'm getting a new brother or sister, but I can't wait for Mom to act normal again," he said.

"What do you mean?" Elizabeth asked.

Andy made a face. "Well, she's tired all the time. And she eats the strangest food."

21

"Like what?" Amy asked. She looked at Elizabeth and grinned. "Pickle ice cream?"

The other kids laughed, but Andy nodded. "Yes! Once she had a bowl of ice cream and a pickle at the same time."

Jessica scrunched up her nose. "Yuck. My mom better not eat that when she gets pregnant."

"Is she going to have a baby?" Eva wanted to know.

The rest of the girls looked surprised, and Jessica shook her head. "Not yet, but Liz and I are going to talk her into it."

"What if she doesn't want another baby?" Amy asked.

"She does," Jessica said. "I can tell." She took a big bite of her tuna fish sandwich and thought about what Andy had said. Her mother had been complaining about being tired lately. Sometimes she even took a nap in the afternoon.

Jessica thought it over some more. Last week her mother had put ketchup *and* mustard on her hamburger. And she had eaten two extra pickles with her meal. Maybe she was *already* pregnant! She could hardly wait to talk to Elizabeth alone.

"Liz," she whispered during math class.

Elizabeth was adding a long column of numbers and didn't look up. She never wanted to talk during class. "What?" she finally whispered back.

"I think Mom really might be having a baby," Jessica said in Elizabeth's ear.

Elizabeth put down her pencil. "What?" she gasped.

24

Jessica nodded. "She has all the right signs, just like Andy was saying."

"What do you mean?" Elizabeth asked. "What signs?"

"She's sleepy all the time," Jessica began. She counted off on her fingers. "Plus, sometimes she eats really funny things. Plus, she keeps talking about the DeVitos' baby like it was the best thing in the world."

"Why wouldn't she have told us?" Elizabeth asked.

"No talking, please," Mrs. Otis said from the front of the room. Elizabeth turned red, but Jessica didn't care. This was too important.

"I don't know why she wouldn't tell us," she whispered. "Maybe she wants it to be a secret for a while."

Elizabeth was looking at her math problems and shaking her head. "I think she would tell us," she said softly.

"I have an idea," Jessica said. "Let's spy on her and see if we find any other signs. Then we'll know for sure."

"That's a good idea," Elizabeth said.

At the same time, they each crossed their hearts and snapped their fingers twice. That was their secret promise signal. They were going to find out if there was a new Wakefield on the way.

CHAPTER 5

Baby Clothes

When they got home from school, Elizabeth and Jessica found their mother in the living room. She was lying down on the couch. Jessica poked Elizabeth with her elbow and widened her eyes. Pregnant women took lots of naps! Elizabeth shook Mrs. Wakefield's shoulder.

"Mom?" she whispered.

"Oh!" Mrs. Wakefield opened her eyes and smiled. "You two were quiet as mice," she said. She held out her arms. "Let me give my baby girls a big hug."

Elizabeth and Jessica both climbed onto the couch with their mother, and had a short tickle fight. Then Elizabeth remembered that her mother might be pregnant, so she stopped tickling her.

"Sorry, Mom," she said.

Mrs. Wakefield laughed. "That's OK. Now that you're home, it's time to go shopping."

"Really?" Jessica said, clapping her hands. "What for?"

"You two need some new school clothes," their mother explained. "Steven has gone over to Mark Morris's house, so we have all afternoon. Let's get going."

Buying clothes was one of the things the twins disagreed on. Jessica loved to shop and Elizabeth hated it. Jessica wanted to try on every dress in every store, and all Elizabeth cared about was picking what she needed. It didn't matter to her what matched what.

The twins did agree that they loved going places after school in the car.

When they arrived at the mall, they spent half an hour trying on shoes and half an hour trying on school clothes. Finally, the twins chose two new outfits each, and Jessica talked their mother into getting them some new barrettes, too.

"I think that's all we need," Mrs. Wakefield announced when they were finished. The three of them were holding hands and walking through the mall.

"We might need some new socks," Jessica said as they walked past a window filled with colorful socks and tights.

Mrs. Wakefield shook her head. "I just bought you two new pairs last week, remember? I got—"

Suddenly, she stopped walking. They were standing in front of a baby boutique. Elizabeth looked up at her mother in surprise. "What is it, Mom?"

"Let's go in here," Mrs. Wakefield said, leading the way into the store.

Jessica glanced at Elizabeth and nodded slowly. Elizabeth stared at their mother. Could it be true?

"Look at how darling these little dresses are," Mrs. Wakefield said. She held up a hanger with a tiny ruffled pink dress on it. "This is simply adorable."

"They look like doll clothes," Jessica agreed, holding up a tiny yellow sweater.

Mrs. Wakefield was smiling. "I think we should get a gift for Mrs. DeVito's new baby," she said. "You girls can help me pick something out."

While Elizabeth looked through the rack of stretchy one-piece suits, Jessica examined each dress carefully. Elizabeth's mind was racing. Everyone seemed to be thinking about babies lately. She wasn't one-hundred-percent sure her mother was pregnant, but there were definitely a lot of clues that she was.

"How about this one?" Jessica said. She held up a white dress with pink hearts on it.

Mrs. Wakefield's eyes sparkled. "It's beautiful," she said tenderly. She turned to Elizabeth. "What did you find?"

Elizabeth pointed to a blue T-shirt-and-

shorts outfit with pictures of building blocks and teddy bears all over it. Their mother let out a gasp.

"That is just the cutest thing I ever saw!" she exclaimed. "I'll have to get both. I'll give one to Mrs. DeVito—"

"What will you do with the other one?" Jessica cut in breathlessly.

Elizabeth could feel her heart pounding. Why did their mother need *extra* baby clothes?

"It can always come in handy," Mrs. Wakefield said. "You never know when you might need it."

When Mrs. Wakefield took the clothes to the cash register, Elizabeth and Jessica stayed by the rack of dresses.

"What do you think?" Jessica whispered excitedly.

Elizabeth glanced at their mother. "I think she might be having a baby."

CHAPTER 6

A List of Names

Jessica sat and daydreamed during spelling and reading class on Friday morning. Thinking about having a new brother or sister made her so excited she couldn't concentrate on school at all. She turned to a fresh page in her notebook and began writing down all the prettiest names she knew.

"Victoria Ashley Melanie Jaqueline Annabel Wakefield," she wrote in her best handwriting. She smiled as she read the names. They sounded perfect to her. She was so positive she would have a baby sister that she didn't bother to put down any boys' names.

"Psst," she said to Elizabeth.

Her sister looked over at her. "What is it?" she asked quietly.

Jessica ripped the page out of the notebook and handed it to her. Elizabeth read the list.

"These are too fancy," she whispered. Elizabeth began writing down her own choices, while Jessica peeked to see what they were.

"Emily Claire Wakefield," Elizabeth wrote.

Jessica sighed. Elizabeth always wanted things to be so simple! She took the list back from her sister and handed it to Lila.

"Write down what you think are the best names," she whispered.

Lila read the list while she chewed on the

end of her pen. "I know," she said. She wrote busily, and then handed the paper back to Jessica.

"Alexandra Cassandra Wakefield" was what Lila had put down.

"Those are nice!" Jessica said.

"What are nice?" Mrs. Otis asked from her desk.

Jessica looked up to see her teacher looking right at her. "Ummm . . ." she mumbled.

"May I have the note, please?" Mrs. Otis asked.

Blushing, Jessica stood up and walked slowly to the front of the room. Mrs. Otis took the paper. "What's this?" she asked with a puzzled smile.

"They're names for our new baby," Jessica explained. She was glad the teacher didn't

seem angry, so she smiled, too. "Our mom is going to have another baby."

"She is?" Mrs. Otis asked in surprise. "That's wonderful news!"

Elizabeth raised her hand. "We're not sure yet. We just think so."

"Well, you be sure to tell us if she really is," Mrs. Otis said. "Now let's get back to work."

Jessica ran back to her seat and grinned at Elizabeth. Maybe her sister wasn't sure, but *she* was. More than anything, Jessica wanted a little sister.

"Let's see if Mom has any more baby clothes at home," Jessica suggested as they walked home from the school bus.

Elizabeth nodded. "Good idea."

They tiptoed into the house and put their

books down. They could hear their mother talking on the telephone. Elizabeth put one finger over her lips.

"Where should we look?" Jessica whispered.

Elizabeth pointed over their heads. "Upstairs."

Without making a sound, they tiptoed up the stairs and into their parents' bedroom. Jessica felt a little bit bad about snooping, but it was for an important reason. She looked around, wondering where to start.

"Hey! Look at this!" Elizabeth gasped.

Jessica ran to Elizabeth, who was standing by Mrs. Wakefield's dresser. On it was her big book of wallpaper patterns. All the designs were of ducks, rainbows, clouds, and other pretty baby designs.

"These are all for baby rooms!" Jessica said.

Elizabeth's eyes were round with surprise. "And look at this other stuff in here," she went on.

There were cut-out pictures of cribs, mobiles, stuffed animals, changing tables, and everything else for the perfect baby's room.

"Do you think Mom picked this stuff out for the guest room?" Elizabeth whispered. "Do you think she's redecorating it for a baby?"

Jessica's heart was racing. She couldn't believe how lucky they were! "That's what it looks like," she agreed happily.

"Then I guess it's true," Elizabeth said.

They looked at each other for a moment. Then they jumped up and down and hugged each other.

"We're having a baby!" Jessica shouted.

CHAPTER 7

Waaaah!

The next morning, the twins had a private conversation before breakfast. "I don't know why Mom hasn't said anything about the baby yet," Elizabeth said.

"Maybe it's a surprise," Jessica suggested.

Elizabeth nodded. "Maybe if we give her hints that we know about it, she'll tell us."

"Good idea," Jessica said. "Come on."

They ran downstairs to the kitchen. Their parents were reading the newspaper and drinking coffee. Jessica nudged Elizabeth to say something.

"We were just talking about Jenny," Elizabeth said. "We think babies are really, really nice."

"That's right," Jessica chimed in. "We love babies."

Mrs. Wakefield smiled. "So do I."

Elizabeth glanced at her sister. Jessica nodded.

"We love taking care of babies, too," Elizabeth said, staring into her mother's eyes.

"And I'm glad to hear you say that," Mrs. Wakefield said. "Remember, Mrs. DeVito said you could go over any time to help with Jenny."

"Could we? We really want to help," Jessica said.

Mr. Wakefield put down his coffee cup. "I

have a good idea. Why don't you go to her house today and offer to help her?"

Elizabeth looked at Jessica again. Their parents still weren't admitting they were having a baby of their own.

"I think that's a very good idea," Mrs. Wakefield said. "Go over after you've had your breakfast."

"OK," Jessica said. She looked at Elizabeth and shrugged. Their hints weren't working.

After breakfast, the twins walked over to the DeVitos' house and knocked on the kitchen door. Mrs. DeVito answered. "Hello, girls."

"We came to help you with Jenny," Elizabeth explained. "In case you need us."

Mrs. DeVito looked very pleased. "Wonderful! Mr. DeVito is working at his office today, and I have a lot of chores to do. Would you baby-sit Jenny while I clean the house?"

They nodded and followed Mrs. DeVito inside. Jenny was sleeping in her basket, sucking on her thumb. Elizabeth thought she looked adorable.

"All you have to do is tell me if she wakes up," Mrs. DeVito said, leaving them alone.

Elizabeth and Jessica sat down and watched Jenny. She didn't do anything but sleep. Upstairs, the vacuum cleaner went on.

"She's very good," Jessica whispered.

Elizabeth nodded.

Jenny opened her mouth and yawned, but she didn't wake up.

"What are we supposed to do?" Jessica asked.

Elizabeth shrugged. "Just watch her, I guess."

And that's what they did for the next half hour. Finally, Jenny opened her eyes.

"Hi, Jenny," Jessica said softly.

Jenny wiggled her legs and started to cry.

"Shh!" Elizabeth said quickly. "Don't cry."

Jenny squeezed her eyes shut. She looked like she was ready to fall asleep again, but then she let out a loud wail.

"What's wrong?" Elizabeth asked.

"I don't know," Jessica said. She was beginning to look worried. Jenny was crying and crying. "We didn't do anything wrong!" Jessica added.

Elizabeth bit her lip. "I'll get Mrs. DeVito."
She ran to the stairs and called. "Jenny
woke up! She's crying!"

Mrs. DeVito hurried down. "Maybe she
needs to be changed," she said. "Would you
like to help?"

Mrs. DeVito took the screaming baby upstairs. Elizabeth and Jessica followed and
watched as Mrs. DeVito undid the diaper.
Jessica held her nose.

"Yuck," Jessica whispered to Elizabeth.
"It's pretty messy."

Elizabeth nodded but didn't say anything.
That part of taking care of babies wasn't very
much fun.

"Now just jiggle the basket if she fusses
again," Mrs. DeVito said when she was done.
"She's just a little cranky today."

When they were downstairs again, Elizabeth and Jessica tried to give Jenny her pacifier, but the baby kept spitting it out and crying.

"This is awful!" Jessica complained. "She won't stop crying!"

Elizabeth put the pacifier into Jenny's mouth again, but it instantly popped out. Jenny's face was red from screaming.

"Rock the basket a little," Elizabeth said.

Jessica started jiggling the basket, but it only made Jenny scream more. Elizabeth felt terrible. They weren't being any help at all. She was about to get Mrs. DeVito again, when Mrs. DeVito came down.

"I'm sorry," Elizabeth said. "We can't get her to stop crying."

"That's OK. That's what babies are like.

Thank you for helping," Mrs. DeVito said. "I guess I won't get any cleaning done today if she's so cranky. But I hope you'll come visit again."

"Sure," Elizabeth said in a doubtful voice.

The twins left and walked back to their house. "Whew," Jessica said. "Cranky is right. I'm glad we could leave."

"Me, too," Elizabeth said. They looked at each other, but didn't say anything more. They were thinking the same thing.

Maybe having a baby in the house wouldn't be so much fun, after all.

CHAPTER 8

On Second Thought

After lunch, the twins changed into their bathing suits and floated on their rafts in the pool. Their father was reading a book in a lawn chair nearby. Jessica paddled close to Elizabeth.

"I was thinking," she said, keeping her voice low.

Elizabeth trailed her fingers in the water. "About what?"

"You know how Mom calls us her baby girls sometimes?" Jessica said. Elizabeth nodded. "Well, if we had a baby sister, we wouldn't be her babies anymore."

"I know," Elizabeth said quietly.

Jessica glanced over at their father. "We would just be older sisters."

"I know," Elizabeth said.

"Steven would be special because he's the oldest, and the baby would be special because it would be the youngest," Jessica went on. "We'd be in the middle."

Elizabeth nodded again. She looked like she was deep in thought.

"Babies are nice," Jessica said, trying to sound positive. "But they're kind of—"

"Noisy," Elizabeth finished for her.

Jessica nodded and made a face. "Yes. And the diapers."

"Yuck. They're pretty awful," Elizabeth said.

"Mom would have to spend a lot of time with the baby," Jessica added.

She paddled her feet in the water and frowned. Spending the morning with Jenny DeVito gave her a lot to think about. There was more to babies than just cuddly bundles to play with and dress up. There was a lot of work, too.

"But babies grow up," Elizabeth reminded Jessica.

Jessica looked at her sister. She wasn't so sure she still wanted a baby sister. She wondered if Elizabeth felt the same way.

"Liz?" she asked. "Do you think Mom is really having a baby?"

Elizabeth bit her lip and looked nervous.

"Ummm. I'm not sure. We found the wall-paper and she bought those extra clothes."

Jessica started remembering all the special things their mother did with them, like going to the park and taking them to modern-dance class. Mrs. Wakefield liked being a class mother on field trips, too, and helping out at school parties. If there was a baby in the house, Mrs. Wakefield wouldn't be able to do a lot of those things anymore. Just thinking about it made Jessica feel sad.

What if they never got to spend time with their mother anymore? A baby would need so much attention. And they would probably have to do extra chores and have to be very quiet all the time. Jessica wasn't ready to give up being the baby of the family yet.

"Liz?" Jessica whispered.

Elizabeth sighed. "What?"

"Do you still wish we had a baby sister—or brother?" Jessica asked.

Elizabeth shook her head. "Not so much, anymore."

"Neither do I," Jessica whispered.

"What if it's too late?" Elizabeth asked.

Jessica gulped. Now what were they going to do?

CHAPTER 9

Worried!

Elizabeth woke up on Sunday morning feeling worried.

She didn't like to admit it, but she no longer wanted a baby sister or brother very much. Babies were nice, but she hoped her mother wouldn't have another one right away.

But what if their mother wanted another baby? What if she thought the twins were getting too old? Maybe their mother wanted a little baby to hug, instead of two old girls.

Elizabeth turned on her side and threw

her stuffed koala bear at Jessica's bed. "Are you awake?" she asked.

Jessica stretched and sat up. "Yes."

"Let's go to Mom and Dad's room," Elizabeth said.

They tiptoed down the hall and peeked into their parents' room. Mr. and Mrs. Wakefield were still asleep. Elizabeth put one finger to her lips and waved to Jessica. They crept quietly to the bed.

"Mom?" Elizabeth whispered. "Can we get in with you?"

Mrs. Wakefield slowly opened her eyes. "Good morning," she said sleepily. She held the covers open. "Climb in."

While Elizabeth and Jessica crawled in under the covers, Mr. Wakefield turned over and mumbled. "We're being invaded," he said.

59

Jessica giggled. "It's just us, Daddy."

Elizabeth and Jessica sat between their parents. Mrs. Wakefield sat up, too. "This is nice and cozy," she said. "I like having my little girls here with me."

"We're your babies, right?" Jessica said.

"Of course," Mrs. Wakefield said.

"And you're very happy with us, right?" Jessica went on.

Their mother laughed. "Of course I am," she said, hugging them. "I think you're the best."

Elizabeth crossed her fingers under the covers. "Don't you think three is a good number of children to have?" she asked.

"*I* do," Jessica answered quickly.

"You know," Mrs. Wakefield said. "When I think of Mrs. DeVito just starting out with one little girl, I think of all the things I learned about being a mom by having three."

Mr. Wakefield chuckled. "Jenny will probably be a lot easier to start with than Steven was."

"She is one of the sweetest babies I've ever seen," Mrs. Wakefield agreed. She sat up and rested her back against the pillow. "Sometimes I wish you two girls were still babies. You're growing up so quickly."

Elizabeth gulped. Did that mean their mother was ready for another one, now? "Babies are a lot of trouble, though," she said quickly. "They make a lot of noise. Jenny cried the whole time we were over there."

"True, but it's worth it," Mrs. Wakefield said.

Elizabeth was getting very upset not knowing if her mother was expecting a baby. Finally, she decided that the only thing to do was ask.

CHAPTER 10

Special Kids

Elizabeth scrambled out of bed, pulling on Jessica's hand. "Follow me," she said.

"Where are we going?" Jessica asked, confused.

Without answering, Elizabeth ran back to their bedroom and shut the door behind Jessica. Then she stood against it.

"What is it?" Jessica asked. She thought her sister was acting strange.

Elizabeth looked very serious. "I think we should just ask them," she said solemnly.

"You mean, just ask?" Jessica whispered. She made a face. "OK. But *you* ask."

Elizabeth nodded. "Come on." She opened the door, and they went back to their parents' room. Both girls stood by the foot of the bed.

"So, you came back," their father teased. "We were wondering what got into you two. You shot out of here like rockets."

Mrs. Wakefield looked curious. "You seem to have something on your minds," she said. "Do you want to talk about anything?"

Jessica poked Elizabeth's foot with her toe. "Go on," she whispered. "Ask."

"Ask what?" Mr. Wakefield said with a smile.

"Mom?" Elizabeth said in a hoarse voice. "Are you—are you—"

"Am I what?" Mrs. Wakefield wanted to know.

"Are you having a baby?" Jessica blurted out.

Nobody spoke. Mr. and Mrs. Wakefield looked at each other, and then at the twins. "What makes you think that?" she asked.

Elizabeth's cheeks were pink. "You have all the signs," she explained. "You're tired all the time—"

"And you bought baby clothes," Jessica added.

"And you're changing the guest room into a nursery," Elizabeth continued. "And you keep saying you love babies so much."

Mr. Wakefield began to chuckle, and then he laughed harder and harder. Mrs. Wakefield poked him in the ribs, and he stopped.

"I thought you loved babies!" Mrs. Wakefield said.

"We do, but—" Jessica didn't finish her sentence. She couldn't understand what was so funny.

Mrs. Wakefield held out her arms, and the twins climbed onto the bed again. She held them on each side of her.

"Now, listen," she began. "The reason I've been tired is because I'm working hard on my decorating class. And those nursery decorations are just part of my homework."

Elizabeth's eyes brightened. "And the extra baby clothes?" she asked.

"I know another woman who is pregnant," their mother said with a laugh. "I love babies, but I'm happy with the family I have."

Jessica felt so happy and relieved that she laughed, too. "So you aren't having another baby?"

"No," their mother said. "Definitely not."

"And you don't think we're getting too old?" Jessica went on.

Their father laughed again. "Definitely not!" he said.

"Of course you're growing up," Mrs. Wakefield said lovingly. "But just because you're not babies anymore doesn't mean we don't still love you."

"Really?" Jessica asked, just to make sure.

Her mother gave her a big hug. "Really. You're all special in your own way. Steven and Elizabeth and Jessica. How could I want more?"

"We'll even love you just as much when

you're grown-up and have kids of your own," Mr. Wakefield said.

Elizabeth smiled. "We were so sure you were pregnant."

Mrs. Wakefield laughed and replied, "You two just jumped to conclusions."

Jessica stood up and jumped to the end of the bed. "Like that," she giggled.

"Exactly," their mother agreed. "Now jump on down and we'll make pancakes for breakfast. And next time you're wondering about something important—"

"We should ask you first," Elizabeth said, finishing the sentence.

After breakfast, Elizabeth and Jessica went out to the front yard and tried to do handstands and cartwheels.

"How was that?" Jessica asked after doing a floppy cartwheel. Her jeans had grass stains on the knees.

"It was OK," Elizabeth said, as she came down from her handstand.

Just then, a soccer ball rolled across the lawn in front of her. She turned around to see who had kicked it.

"Sorry!" Todd Wilkins called. He ran up the sidewalk and picked up his soccer ball.

"Where are you going?" Elizabeth asked him.

Todd bounced the soccer ball on his knee a few times. "I'm going over to Ken's house," he answered. "We're practicing for soccer league tryouts."

"When are the tryouts?" Elizabeth asked eagerly.

"Next week," Todd said. He kicked his soccer ball back to the sidewalk.

"Can anybody try out?" Elizabeth called, running after him. Todd turned back. "Sure. Do you want to try out?" he said. "Are you sure you're good enough?"

"I'm good enough!" Elizabeth shouted back.

Todd kicked his soccer ball down the street.

"We'll see," he said. "There's going to be some pretty stiff competition."

Elizabeth felt angry. She was just as good in soccer as anyone else, and no one was going to stop her from trying out if she wanted to.

Will Elizabeth make the soccer team? Find out in Sweet Valley Kids #15, Fearless Elizabeth.

71

SWEET VALLEY KIDS

Jessica and Elizabeth have had lots of adventures in *Sweet Valley High* and *Sweet Valley Twins*...now read about the twins at age seven! You'll love all the fun that comes with being seven—birthday parties, playing dress-up, class projects, putting on puppet shows and plays, losing a tooth, setting up lemonade stands, caring for animals and much more! It's all part of SWEET VALLEY KIDS. Read them all!